Max Velthuijs (1923–2005) was born in The Hague, Netherlands. As a toddler he loved to draw and make up his own stories. After studying painting and graphic design, he went on to become one of the most famous illustrators for children in The Netherlands and received many awards. In 2004 he received the Hans Christian Andersen Award for illustrators.

Copyright © 1969 by NordSüd Verlag AG, CH-8050 Zürich, Switzerland.
First published in Switzerland under the title *Junge und der Fisch*.
English translation copyright © 1969, 2018 by NorthSouth Books.

This edition published in the United States, Great Britain, Canada, Australia,
and New Zealand in 2018 by NorthSouth Books, Inc., an imprint of NordSüd Verlag AG,
CH-8005 Zürich, Switzerland.

Illustration: © 2005 by Foundation Max Velthuijs
Text: © 2005 by Foundation Max Velthuijs

Distributed in the United States by NorthSouth Books, Inc., New York 10016.
Library of Congress Cataloging-in-Publication Data is available.
ISBN: 978-0-7358-4309-7
Printed in Latvia
1 3 5 7 9 • 10 8 6 4 2
www.northsouth.com

The Little Boy and the Big Fish

written and illustrated by Max Velthuijs

North
South

For my cat

Once upon a time there was a boy who lived in the country with his mother, a cat, some chickens, and a rooster. He loved to go fishing. Sometimes he caught one or two fish, but most of the time he dreamed about catching a great big fish.

Early one morning he took his fishing rod and went down to the lake to try his luck. It was a fine day, and when he reached the water's edge he found a comfortable place, baited his hook, and begin to fish.

He waited. And he waited. Will the big fish come? The water was still and the weather was just right for fishing.

The sound of the humming bees filled the air. Butterflies darted about overhead and the birds sang. A little beetle crawled toward the boy. But no fish came.

Perhaps the fish were not hungry. But the boy was! He fixed his fishing rod to the ground and began to eat, never taking his eyes off the float on the water. He ate bread and butter and an apple, and had a big drink of milk. Then he felt sleepy, so he lay down on the grass, close his eyes, and dreamed about a great big fish.

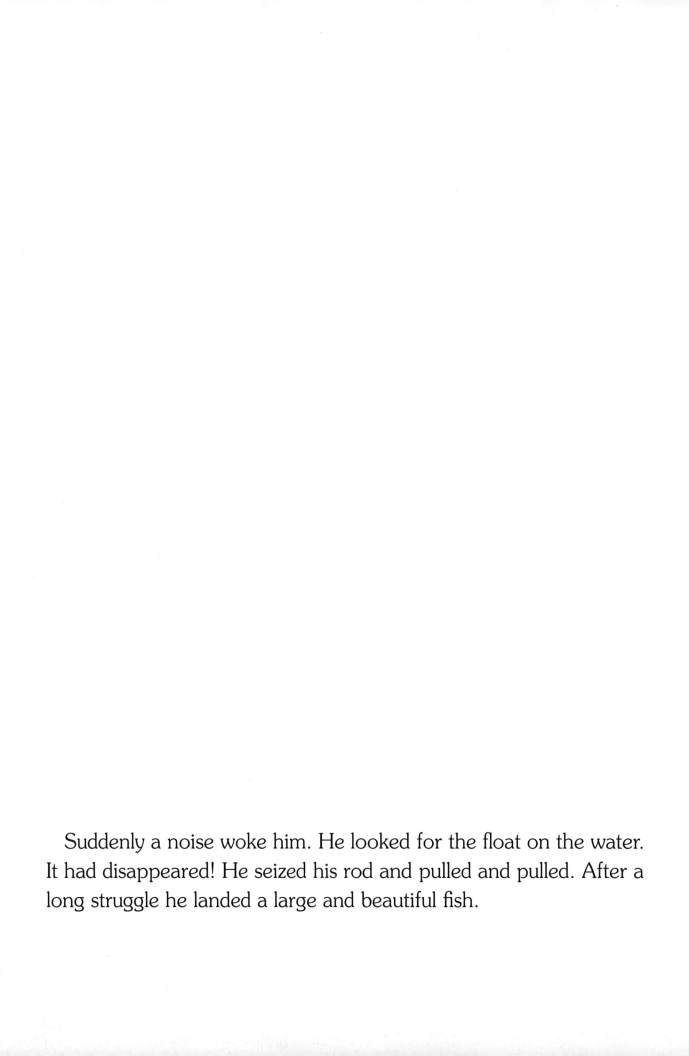

Suddenly a noise woke him. He looked for the float on the water. It had disappeared! He seized his rod and pulled and pulled. After a long struggle he landed a large and beautiful fish.

He could not believe his eyes! He put the fish under his arm and hurried off home.

On the way, he met a farmer who said, "I'll buy that fish from you. It'll be just right for dinner."

But the boy did not want to sell. "Nobody will eat my fish," he replied. "I want him to live and be happy."

His mother was amazed when she saw how big the fish was. "He's beautiful, but he will soon die out of water," she said.

"Perhaps he could live in the bathtub," said the boy. Quickly his mother filled the tub with water. The boy put the fish in, but he was so large he could not move. He lay there, quite still.

He looked sad, and this made the boy sad too. He said to the fish, "I will go and fetch some flowers to put beside the tub so that you will feel more at home." When he had done that, he read to the fish. He chose nice stories about animals. The fish seem to listen, but still he was unhappy.

The next morning the fish was pale and did not want to eat. The boy, who by now loved him dearly, took him to the doctor.

The doctor put him on the table and gently opened his mouth. "He has caught a cold," he said, and tied a bandage around his throat. The doctor gave the boy a bottle of medicine. *One spoonful three times a day* was written on the label.

Then the boy hurried home through the town, with the fish under his arm.

The fish had never seen a town before. The traffic and the crowds of people frightened him, but he trusted the boy.

As soon as they reached home the boy put the fish back in the bathtub and immediately gave him a dose of the medicine. The fish was glad to be back in the water. *Tomorrow I'll be quite well again*, he thought, and with hope in his heart, he fell asleep.

And as he slept he dreamed that his fins became wings. He flew out of the window. He saw the little house and the trees below. Above him the moon was shining.

Then he saw the lake, his old home. Joyfully he flew down toward it. He felt cool water lapping around him and he awoke, only to find that he was in the bathtub. The beautiful dream was over.

Early the next morning the boy came with the bottle of medicine. He asked the fish how he felt. The fish looked at the boy longingly, and the expression in his eyes said, *I do not think there is anything wrong with me, but I am homesick for my lake. Please, please take me back there, for I shall never be happy in a bathtub.*

The boy understood, and because he loved the fish so much, he decided to give him back his freedom.

Very early the next morning he took the fish under his arm and made his way across the field to the lake.

At the water's edge the boy said good-bye to his friend and put him gently into the water.

And when he saw how happy the fish was as he swam away, flipping his fins, he was happy too.

The Kind-hearted Monster
Two classic stories by Max Velthuijs—
Hans Christian Andersen Award-winning illustrator!
ISBN: 978-0-7358-4107-9

What do you do with a fire-breathing monster? Adore him! When the people of a little town discover that the fire-breathing monster in their midst is really a kind-hearted, mild-mannered monster, they all have different ideas about what to do with him. But the ideas make Mervyn unhappy, until a professor has an idea that lightens everyone's mood—especially Mervyn's! In "The Monster and the Robbers" … Robbers have kidnapped Mervyn the monster by baking him cakes full of sleeping powder. They think the heist is a success. But the robbers don't know Mervyn … and the people from the town that's halfway to nowhere.

"With enduring themes of acceptance and kindness, these stories will charm a new generation."—*School Library Journal*